A Thousand Y(

A Romance of the Orient

Percy MacKaye

Alpha Editions

This edition published in 2023

ISBN : 9789357946520

Design and Setting By
Alpha Editions
www.alphaedis.com
Email - info@alphaedis.com

THE AUTHOR

Percy MacKaye, the author of this play, was born in New York City, March 16, 1875—a son of Steele MacKaye. He graduated from Harvard with the class of 1897 and shortly afterward spent two years in Italy and at the University of Leipzig. In 1904 he joined the Cornish (New Hampshire) Colony and has since devoted himself to literary and dramatic work. He is a member of the National Institute of Arts and Letters.

Following is a list of his published works:

- THE CANTERBURY PILGRIMS: A Comedy.

- THE CANTERBURY TALES OF CHAUCER.

- FENRIS, THE WOLF: A Tragedy.

- JEANNE D'ARC: A Tragedy.

- SAPPHO AND PHAON: A Tragedy.

- THE SCARECROW: A Tragedy of the Ludicrous.

- LINCOLN CENTENARY ODE.

- MATER: An American Study in Comedy.

- THE PLAYHOUSE AND THE PLAY. Essays.

- A GARLAND TO SYLVIA: A Comedy.

- ANTI-MATRIMONY: A Satirical Comedy.

- YANKEE FANTASIES. Five One-Act Plays.

- TO-MORROW. A Play in Three Acts.

- POEMS.

- URIEL, AND OTHER POEMS.

- THE CIVIC THEATRE.

- SANCTUARY: A Bird Masque.

- A THOUSAND YEARS AGO.

Original Cast of the Play as first produced in Boston, at the Shubert Theatre, December 1, 1913

WILLIAM A. BRADY (LTD.)

PRESENTS

A THOUSAND YEARS AGO

A Romance of the Orient

BY

PERCY MACKAYE

"Here in China, the world lies a-dream, like a thousand

Years ago, and the place of our dreams is eternal."

(The play is an original comedy, suggested by the Persian romance in "The Thousand and One Tales," wherein is recited the adventures of Calaf, Prince of Astrakhan, and the beautiful Princess of China.)

CAST OF CHARACTERS

ASIATIC

TURANDOT, Princess of Pekin	Rita Jolivet
ALTOUM, her father, Emperor	Frederick Warde
ZELIMA, her slave	Fania Marinoff
CALAF, Prince of Astrakhan	Jerome Patrick
BARAK, his servitor	Frank McCormack
CHANG, Eunuch	Edmund Roth

EUROPEAN

SCARAMOUCHE		Sheldon Lewis
PUNCHINELLO	Vagabond Players from Italy	Bennett Kilpack
PANTALOON		Allen Thomas
HARLEQUIN		Joseph Smith

CAPOCOMICO, their leader	H. Cooper Cliffe

LORDS OF THE ROYAL DIVAN

Hugh Nixon, John P. Savage, Anthony Romack, Reginald Simpson

BEGGARS

William H. Dupont and W. Bradley Ward

SOLDIERS OF PEKIN

David Earle, Charles Muche, Thomas Edwards, Joseph Reed, Howard
Jackson, Carl Textoris, Joseph Weston, James Bannister

TEA BEARERS

Franklin Montgomery and John Leons

COURT ATTENDANTS

Philip Sheridan and Robert W. Gest

FEMALE ATTENDANTS

Marie Benton, Daisy Miller, Ruth Pierson, Constance Howard, Elsie Oates
and Sybil Maitland

SCENES

ACT I

City Gate at Pekin

ACT II

Scene 1: Room in the Imperial Harem

Scene 2: Great Hall of the Emperor

ACT III

Scene 1: Turandot's Dream

(1) The Mountains

(2) A Street

Scene 2: Anteroom of the Harem

Scene 3: Calaf's Bedchamber

ACT IV

Great Hall of the Emperor. (The same as Act II, Scene 2)

Play produced under the direction of Mr. J. C. Huffman

Interpretative music composed by William Furst

EXECUTIVE STAFF

Tarkington Baker	Manager
Frederick Schader	Business Manager
Frank McCormack	Stage Director
William W. Brown W. Bradley Ward	Stage Managers
William Furst	Musical Director

PREFACE

The present play is an original comedy, of which certain elements in the plot have been suggested by the old Persian tale which is the theme of the eighteenth century Italian comedy "Turandotte," by Carlo Gozzi, translated into German by Friedrich Schiller.

It is not a revision or rewriting of that work.

It is an entirely new play.

Since, however, some modern productions have recently been made in Germany, England and America, under the title of "Turandot," it is fitting to make clear the relation which my play bears to those and to the older productions of Gozzi and Schiller.

In January, 1762, "Turandotte" by Carlo Gozzi was first acted by the Sacchi company of players at Venice. It was one of a number of "improvised comedies"—or *Commedie dell' Arte Improvisata*—composed by Gozzi in his single-handed artistic war against the more naturalistic works of Goldoni, his contemporary.

The plots of these comedies, or *Fiabe*, were derived from nursery or folk-tales. They were acted by masked, or semi-masked players. Their technique was based on the old Italian form of *scenari*. This form is described by John Addington Symonds, in the Preface to his "Memories of Count Carlo Gozzi," as follows:

"Comparative study of these *scenari* shows that the whole comedy was planned out, divided into acts and scenes, the parts of the several personages described in prose, their entrances and exits indicated, and what they had to do laid down in detail. The execution was left to the actors; and it is difficult to form a correct conception of the acted play from the dry bones of its *ossatura*. 'Only one thing afflicts me,' said our Marston in the Preface to his *Malcontent*: 'to think that scenes invented merely to be spoken, should be inforcively published to be read.' And again in his Preface to the *Fawne*: 'Comedies are writ to be spoken, not read; remember the life of these things consists in action.' If that was true of pieces composed in dialogue by an English playwright of the Elizabethan age, how far more true is it of the skeletons of comedies, which avowedly owed their force and spirit to extemporaneous talent! Reading them, we feel that we are viewing the machine of stakes and irons which a sculptor sets up before he begins to mould the figure of an athlete or a goddess in plastic clay.

"The *scenario*, like the *plat* described for us by Malone and Collier, was hung up behind the stage. Every actor referred to it while the play went forward, refreshing his memory with what he had to represent, and attending to his entrances."

Written as *scenari* Gozzi's acted *Fiabe* were eminently successful in their day, and established his works as models of a dramatic taste which, toward the last of the eighteenth century, it became the desire of cultivated Germans to introduce into their own country.

With this object in view, Goethe and Schiller selected "Turandotte" as a foreign comedy worthy to be translated and adapted for production at the Weimar Theatre. Accordingly Schiller recast in poetic form a German version of Gozzi's play, made by Werthes, and produced it at Weimar, in honor of the birthday of the Grand Duchess, wife of Karl August, on January 30, 1804. In details of this recasting he was assisted by Goethe.

The attempt, however, thus to "elevate the taste of the German public" was not successful.

More than one hundred years later, Dr. Max Reinhardt produced in Berlin a play based on Schiller's "Turandot" made by Karl Voellmueller. In 1912 an English translation of this version by Jethro Bithell was produced in America by the Shubert Theatrical Company, and after a brief run on the road was withdrawn from the stage. In January, 1913, it was also produced for a short run in London by Sir George Alexander.

Considering the version as it stood to be in need of changes for their purposes, the owners of the American rights requested me to suggest and make the changes. To this I replied that to make alterations or adaptations of the version did not appeal to me, but if the owners would like to give me entire freedom to write a new and original play on the theme of the Persian folk-tale used by Gozzi suitable to the scenic settings of Reinhardt's production, I should be glad to do so. This freedom was courteously given, and the present play was written in the late spring and early summer of this year, and placed in rehearsal in October.

In writing my play, then, I have used for my own purposes the folk-tale material treated differently by Gozzi, and in so doing I have entirely reconceived the story and its situations, omitting many characters of the old tale, introducing and creating several new ones, and characterizing all from a fresh standpoint.[1]

The chief male character of my play, for instance, Capocomico, is wholly new. The name is that which was given to the director or choregus of the old Italian troupes of the *Commedia dell' Arte*, concerning which Symonds writes in his Preface before referred to:

"The Choregus was usually the Capo Comico, or the first actor and manager of the company. He impressed his comrades with a certain unity of tone, brought out the talents of promising comedians, enlarged one part, curtailed another, and squared the piece to be performed with the capacities he could control. 'When a new play has to be given,' says another writer on this subject, 'the first actor calls the troupe together in the morning. He reads them out the plot, and explains every detail of the intrigue. In short, he acts the whole piece before them, points out to each player what his special business requires, indicates the customary sallies of wit and traits of humor, and shows how the several parts and talents of the actors can be best combined into a striking work of scenic art.'"

The four "Maskers" of my play, followers of Capocomico, are, of course, my own renderings of the types familiar to the old Italian comedies.

For their dialogue in the introductory scene of this modern comedy in English, I have invented for them (or rather made use of, for the first time, for modern actors) a form of spoken verse suggestive perhaps of the voluble, capricious, unnaturalistic spirit of fantasy common to them: embodied especially in their leader and spokesman, Capocomico.

Needless to say, "A Thousand Years Ago" historically speaking, there were no disciples of the school of *la Commedia dell' Arte* to invade old China, but fantasy and comedy are older (and younger) than the schools. As Capocomico himself remarks to Punchinello:

"Here is China the world lies a-dream, like a thousand

Years ago, and the place of our dreams is eternal."

To the stage production of the play Mr. J. C. Huffman has brought the admirable powers of his vital directorship.

The theatrical rights are owned and reserved by the Shubert Theatrical Company, of New York.

PERCY MACKAYE.

CORNISH, NEW HAMPSHIRE, November, 1913.

INTRODUCTORY NOTE

The author, in his preface, has explained the pedigree of *"A Thousand Years Ago."* It is the chief advantage of long pedigrees that they allure us from the contemplation of the present to the investigation of the past; and, for students of dramatic literature, perhaps the most important feature of this present play is that the tracing of its ancestry leads us back to one of the most interesting periods in the history of the theatre.

In his quotations from John Addington Symonds, the great English authority on the Renaissance in Italy, Mr. MacKaye has already set before us the main features of the *Commedia dell' Arte Improvisata*, which flourished in Italy for several centuries; but a few additional notes may be appended for the benefit of those who wish to extend their study of this type of drama. Two books upon the subject are readily accessible and may be strongly recommended. One of these is the *"Histoire du Théatre Italien"* by Louis Riccoboni, and the other is a volume entitled *"Masques et Bouffons"* by Maurice Sand, the son of Georges Sand, the famous novelist. Both of these books contain interesting illustrations of the stock characters in Italian comedy; and the pictures in *"Masques el Bouffons"* are reproduced in colors.

The *Commedia dell' Arte* attained its climax about the year 1600, but its career was extended well along into the eighteenth century by the interested activity of the very fertile and very popular playwright, Carlo Gozzi. The essential feature of this type of drama was that the lines were improvised by the actors as they worked their way through the scenes of an intrigue which had been carefully plotted in advance. Throughout the seventeenth century in Italy, the general public showed little patience with the *Commedia Erudita* (the phrase may be translated into contemporary slang as "High-brow drama"), in which the lines were written out by a man of letters and repeated by the actors parrotwise. Such plays, though they might have been composed by poets as eminent as Torquato Tasso, were condemned by the populace because they lacked what seemed the essential element of spontaneity. It will not be difficult for us to understand the attitude of the Italian public toward this distinction, if we apply a similar test to our own contemporary art of after-dinner speaking. We demand of our after-dinner speakers that they shall cull their phrases as they go along, and we respond with dulness to a speech that has been evidently written out and learned by rote. The president of one of our great American universities has been quoted as saying that any professor who writes and learns a lecture is merely insulting the printing-press; there can be no advantage in speaking on a subject unless the speaking be spontaneous: and this was the attitude of the old Italian public toward the actors that addressed it from the stage.

A single set sufficed for most of the improvised Italian comedies. This set represented a public square in an Italian town, a meeting-point of several streets; and the houses of the leading characters were solidly built with doors and windows fronting on the square. With the action set in such a public place, the playwright could experience no embarrassment in motivating his entrances and exits; any characters could meet at any time in the neutral ground of the stage; and the practicable doors and windows of the surrounding houses could be employed by acrobatic actors in the exhibition of exciting scenes of elopement or of robbery.

One of the most definitive features of the *Commedia dell' Arte* was the fact that, though the plays presented differed greatly from each other in subject-matter and in plot, they invariably employed the same set of characters. The individual actor appeared in many different plays, wearing always the same costume and the same mask. Harlequin made love to Columbine in play after play; the Doctor, from Bologna University, repeated the same sort of pedantries in plot after plot; and the Captain Spavento (a lineal descendant of the *Miles Gloriosus* of Plautus) swaggered through story after story. Individual actors became so completely identified with the stock characters they assumed upon the stage that they bore in private life the conventional names of their impersonations. A letter is extant which was sent by Henry Fourth of France (the gallant Henri Quatre of Navarre) to a famous actor of Italy inviting him to bring his company to Paris; and this letter is simply addressed to Harlequin, since the royal patron had no knowledge of the actor's actual name. Similarly, the famous Scarramuccia from whom the immortal Molière learned the rudiments of his craft as a comedian—an actor described in a rhymed chronicle of the time as *"le roi des comédiens et le comédien de rois"*—has come down to us in history under the title of Scaramouche, with no recollection of his parental name.

The modern stage exhibits many analogies to this identification of an actor with a single *rôle*. For instance, in the old days of the association of Weber and Fields, these comedians always appeared in precisely the same parts, regardless of any difference of subject-matter in the comic scenes that they presented. Mr. Weber invariably depicted a fat little man who was easily gullible; and the leaner and more strenuous Mr. Fields was forever getting the better of him and using him as a butt for ridiculous persecution. At the present time, Mr. William Collier approaches very nearly the method of the old Italian actors. Regardless of the particular points of any play in which he chooses to appear, he always represents precisely the same character—a perennial dramatization of his individual traits as a comedian; and he also habitually exercises the Italian actor's license of improvisation in the presence of an assembled audience.

Five of these standard acting types of the *Commedia dell' Arte* are revivified by Mr. MacKaye in his new play on Gozzi's old theme. The most interesting figure is the Capocomico—the leader of the *troupe*, who devises the *scenari* of the plays which they present and rehearses the other actors in the business of their respective parts. This creation of the author's is an evocation of a famous figure from a nigh-forgotten page of the storied past of the theatre, and may serve easily as a starting point for a series of very interesting researches undertaken by individual students of the history of the drama.

Though Mr. MacKaye's play has been written appropriately in English verse, aptly varied in its forms to be spoken by the modern actor, the reader should remember that this drama is designed to appeal more emphatically to the eye than to the ear. It should be regarded as a modification of that type of Decorative Drama which was exhibited by Professor Reinhardt in his masterly production of the pantomime of *"Sumurûn."* For his background, Mr. MacKaye has chosen an old tale of the Arabian Nights which is hung before the eye as a fantastic bit of oriental tapestry; and in the foreground he has exhibited in *silhouette* the sharper colors of the prancing figures of his group of Italian comedians.

More subtly, this play may be conceived as a parabolic comment on a problem of the theatre at the present time. The histrionic disciples of Carlo Gozzi, the eighteenth century champion of traditional romance, are depicted as having lost their fight in Venice against the dramatist Goldoni, who, as a follower of Molière, was regarded at that time as the leader of the realistic movement; and, despairing of being accepted any longer in the country of their birth, these romantic outcasts have sought refuge in the distant orient, an orient to be considered in no sense as historic or realistic, but as purely fantastic. At the present time, our theatre has been conquered (for the moment) by sedulous recorders of the deeds of here and now; we find the drama in the throes of a new realism, more potent in its actuality than the tentative and groping realism of Goldoni; and our romantic playwrights, like these old adventurous and tattered histrions of Carlo Gozzi, have recently sought refuge in the fabulous and eye-enchanting orient. Hence the success, in recent seasons, of such romantic compositions as *"Kismet"* and *"Sumurûn"* and *"The Yellow Jacket."* To escape from the obsession of Broadway and the Strand we now turn eagerly to the gorgeous east, just as these discarded comedians of Gozzi's sought a new success within the enchanting and alluring gates of the city of Pekin.

Furthermore, by restoring to our stage the old European tradition of masks in his group of "Maskers," Mr. MacKaye flings a prophetic shaft in the age-long tourney between symbolism and naturalism in the arts of the theatre.

CLAYTON HAMILTON.

CHARACTERS

Asiatic

TURANDOT	Princess of Pekin
ALTOUM	Her father, Emperor
ZELIMA	Her slave
CALAF	Prince of Astrakhan
BARAK	His servitor
CHANG	Eunuch

European

SCARAMOUCHE

PUNCHINELLO

PANTALOON

Vagabond Players from Italy

HARLEQUIN [Mute]

CAPOCOMICO	Their leader

SCENES

ACT I.

City Gate at Pekin.

ACT II.

Scene 1: Room in the Imperial Harem.
Scene 2: Great Hall of the Emperor.

ACT III.

Scene 1: Anteroom of Harem.
Scene 2: Calaf's Bedchamber.

ACT IV.

Great Hall of the Emperor.
[The same as Act II, Scene 2.]

ACT FIRST

Outside a city gate, at Pekin.

Above the gate, in a row, severed heads of young men are impaled on stakes. On the wall, at one side, more heads of older men, with grizzled locks, stare down: among them, conspicuous, one with a white beard.

It is early morning; the sun just rising.

The gate is closed.

From behind is heard barbaric martial music.

Outside, from the right, drums roll, and Chinese soldiers enter, accompanied by a few beggars and peasants.

Pausing before the gate, they sound a trumpet.

The gate is opened and they pass within, followed by all, except two beggars, a young man and a middle aged.

The gate remains open.

The middle-aged beggar points upward at the head with the white beard.

The younger starts, and prostrates himself beneath it with a deep cry.

Outside, on the left, a twanging of stringed instruments sounds faint but merry. It draws nearer, and quickly the players come running on—five tattered, motley vagabonds in masks: Scaramouche, Harlequin, Punchinello, Pantaloon and Capocomico.

The last, leading them with his baton, stops in the gateway, before which Harlequin executes a ballet-step dance, while Scaramouche, Pantaloon, and Punchinello play accompaniment on guitar, mandolin and zither.

Breaking off, Punchinello begins to improvise an imitation of Harlequin's dance, but being beaten over his hump with a thwacking stick by Harlequin, retreats with grotesque pantomime.

At their merriment, the younger beggar, rising, draws away with the elder, making a tragic gesture toward the white-bearded head on the wall.

Perceiving them, Capocomico silences the musicians and approaches the younger beggar curiously.

Stepping between them, the older beggar salaams and asks alms.

Laughing, Capocomico turns his empty pouch wrong-side-out and bows obsequiously, extending his own palm.

The other Maskers do likewise, sticking out their tongues.

Shrinking from them, the younger beggar draws the older away with him, and goes off, left.

CAPOCOMICO

[*Waving them adieu*]

Mohammed, Confucius, Buddha, befriend you!—

[*Turning to his troupe*]

Behold, my cronies, beggars—beggars
Bow down to us! Lo, they take us for lordlings!
Ha, what did I tell you? Our tables are turning:
In China henceforward we shall be emperors.

SCARAMOUCHE

By the carcase of Charlemagne, I'm dog-aweary
Of twanging these gutstrings for breakfast.

PANTALOON

And us, too,
Of dancing from Venice to Pekin, for sixpence.—
My slippers need soling.

PUNCHINELLO

My poor hump is hollow!

CAPO.

Our journey is ended! Nimble Sir Harlequin,

[*Bowing to each*]

My lord Pantaloon, signore Punchinello,
Magnificent Scaramouche—enter your Kingdom!

- 14 -

SCARAMOUCHE

Enter it!—Now, by the eye-balls of Argus
Where is this same kingdom, Signore Capocomico?
My kingdom is Breakfast: Show me the gateway!

CAPO.

[*Pointing*]

Behold it before you! Within there, the table
Of Fortune is spread for us, served by her handmaids—
Miming Romance, seductive Adventure,
Amorous Magic—improvised Comedy,
And all the love-charming, blood-thirsting Enchantments
Our prosy old workaday world has lost wind of.

SCARAMOUCHE

Ha, beard of Balshazzar! that warms me a bellyful!
'Twas all for the likes of such merry contraptions
We were kicked out of Europe.

CAPO.

Precisely, my bully-boy!
What would you?—At home, half the world is dyspeptic
With pills of reformers and critics and realists.
Fun for its own sake?—Pho, it's old-fashioned!
Art with a mask on?—Unnaturalistic,
They warn you, and scowl, and wag their sad periwigs.—
So *we*—the unmatched, immortal, Olympian
Maskers of Antic,—we, troop of the tragical,
Symbolical, comical, melodramatical
Commedia dell' Arte—we, once who by thousands

Enchanted to laughter the children of Europe—
Behold us now, packed out of town by the critics
To wander the world, hobble-heel, tatter-elbowed,
Abegging our way—four vagabond-players,
And one master director—me, Capocomico!

PUNCHINELLO

But why did you fetch us to China?

CAPO.

Because, my
Punchinello, in China there are no technicians
To measure our noses and label them false ones,
Or question our subplots and call them fictitious.
Here in China the world lies a-dream, like a Thousand
Years Ago, and the place of our dreams is eternal.
Here in China Romance still goes masquing serenely
With dragons, magicians, clowns, villains and heroes,
So that five motley fellows like us may resume our
Old tradetricks, and follow our noses to fortune!—
For a taste point your own, Punch, up there at the gate-stone!

PUNCHINELLO

[*Staring up at the heads*]

What pretty young princes!—But where are the rest of them?

SCARAMOUCHE

By Saladin! They've plenty of room for their breakfast!

PANTALOON

It makes me light-headed to look at them.

CAPO.

Comrades,

Consider, I ask you, where else but in China

May an audience view so romantic a prologue?

These gentlemen open the comedy: Yonder

Behold, in the sunrise, they flaunt their grim Secret

For us to unravel:—Who are they? What means it

That here, on a gateway of Pekin, these gory

Oracular heads stare downward in silence?

And yonder—those others? Who's he in the white beard?—

Love, jealousy, murder—what is their mystery?

By the ghost of old Gozzi, now what are we good for

Unless we untangle their shadowy intrigues!—

Follow *me*, then, my playboys! Before the next sunrise

Your pouches shall burst with the gold of their Secret.—

Follow me!—Yonder heads are our mascots to fortune!

[*Striking their instruments and running through the gate, they all disappear within. As their tinklings die away, the two beggars reënter, from the left*]

THE YOUNGER BEGGAR

[*Prostrating himself again before the white bearded head, rises with up-lifted arms*]

Father!—O slaughtered King of Astrakhan,

Timur, my father!—

THE OLDER BEGGAR

[*Furtively*]

Calaf! Have more care;

There may be ears to listen.

CALAF

[*Distractedly*]

Let them hear!—
Oh, he has held me, Barak, on his knee,
And as a little boy I clutched that beard
With playful fingers: golden brown it was
In those days, and the first bright silver hair
When I had found and plucked it out—, his eyes—
Oh, those poor staring eyes!—they laughed with light,
And with those mummied lips,—red, then, as wine—
He kissed my cheek, and his warm, happy tears
Wet my own face, childish with wonder.—Ah,
My father!

BARAK

Hush! The soldiers of Altoum
Surround us here.

CALAF

Altoum! damned emperor
Of China—I will be avenged on him
Who killed my father, and destroyed our kingdom!

BARAK

And what are you to be avenged on him?—
A beggar.

CALAF

I am prince of Astrakhan!

BARAK

No longer; he is dead. Remember, prince,

How you were drowned a year ago. That night

Altoum destroyed your capitol in war,

You leaped in flight into the river Yen

And perished there.—Do not forget.

CALAF

Forget?

Forget that night? That night I died indeed,

And rose from out the river's chilly death

Into strange paradise: A garden, walled

With roses round: A moon, that zoned with pearl

A spirit there: a lady, garbed in gold

And her more golden smile! Wrapt in disguise—

A beggar's cloak, which you had hid me in,

The river's ooze still staining me with slime—

On me—*me*, outcast and destroyed, she smiled,

And tossed for alms the white rose from her hair!—

[*Taking from his bosom a withered rose, he looks on it rapturously*]

My deathless rose!

BARAK

The rose of Turandot

Is dangerous as her smile.

CALAF

Ah, were it not

That Turandot is daughter of Altoum,

I would have been avenged before to-day.—
But he who killed my father—is her father,
And she is more than life or death, and mightier
Even than a father dead and unavenged:
She is love.

BARAK

Ah, desperate boy, you nurse this love
On worse than poison. Calaf, hark to me.
Have I not served you and your royal father
Faithfully?

CALAF

More than faithfully: lovingly.

BARAK

Then by my love of you, I beg you, boy,
Crush your mad love for Turandot, which must
Lead only to your death, and hasten with me
Far from your enemy's city.

CALAF

My enemy's?

BARAK

Altoum, if he should find you living, would
Spike your head—yonder. Ah, be wise, my prince!
Root out this rashness. Throw that rose away.
See, it is withered—dead. So let your love be!

CALAF

[*Smiling*]

Only a lover rightly loves the rose!
Withered, you tell me?—dead? How dull is the sense
Which does not feel the soul! For me, Barak,
This flower still blooms, and round it all the air
Is sweet with spirit-perfume, even to swooning.

BARAK

[*Rising*]

Then it is vain.—My middle age has lost
Its smell for magic. Well, then, I must be
Content to play the beggar with my prince.

CALAF

Yes, it is vain. For, still I'll wear her rose,
And, in this beggar's cloak she smiled upon,
Still haunt her perilous city.—I have heard
This morning she shall pass this eastern gate
Coming from the palace.—So, my old dear friend,
Wait with me here, for I can only live
By feeding on the glimpses of her face.

BARAK

Come, then, this way and beg, for folk are coming.

[*They draw toward the gate. Barak, starting fearfully, drags Calaf away left*]

Great heaven—the emperor!

CALAF

The emperor!

Wait, Barak. Stop!—No further.

[*On the edge of the scene, they crouch by the wall, like beggars. Through the gate enter Altoum amid Chinese courtiers, accompanied by Capocomico and followed by the other Maskers*]

ALTOUM

[*To Capocomico*]

An instant is enough

For inspiration, and you have inspired

Fresh hopes in me.

CAPO.

That is my specialty,

Your majesty.

ALTOUM

Yet it is strangely sudden:—

You and your motley troop spring in my path

Like gorgeous mushrooms from exotic soils,

And tempt me by your brilliance and surprise

To taste your newness.—Well, I am desperate:

Old remedies have lost their tonic; home

Physicians have proved quacks. I know them all

You—I know not. Therefore I will accept

Your services.

CAPO.

We are practitioners

In every specialty, my liege. If we
Fail to perform our utmost promise—well,

[*Pointing to the gate*]

Our heads are decorative; they will adorn
Your majesty's collection.

ALTOUM

Nay, not mine.
Those grizzled heads of warriors on the wall
Are mine: the trophies of my victories.
But those above the gate—those youthful brows
Of tragic lovers, hapless in their love—
Those are my daughter's.

BARAK

[*To Calaf*]

Do you hear, my prince?
His daughter's! Oh, take heed!

CAPO.

Your majesty
Allures me. Is your daughter—

ALTOUM

Hush! Come closer.

[*He leads Capocomico away from the curtain, right. Calaf follows furtively, heedless of Barak's gestures*]

My daughter is my cause of desperation.
In all but her I have been fortunate:

In peace, most prosperous; in war, my worst
Of rivals, Timur, king of Astrakhan—

[*Pointing at the wall*]

Yonder you see his head! None of his house
Survives to avenge him, for his only son
Perished by drowning.

CALAF

[*To Barak, who implores him to draw back*]

God! if I remain,
I'll kill him.

BARAK

[*Drawing him away*]

Come!

[*They go within the gate*]

CAPO.

Was this long since, my liege?

ALTOUM

This day one year ago.—Some months I kept
Old Timur caged before I bleached him there.—
And strangely it was on that very night
I conquered Astrakhan the change began.

CAPO.

The change—my liege!—what change?

ALTOUM

In Turandot,
My daughter. Always till that time her mind
Was tender-mannered as her face is fair.
Till then, there was no creature living whom
She would have harmed, even with a thought of pain—
Least of all those who loved her. But that night,
Groping by moonlight from her rose garden
Into my war tent, half distractedly
She forced from me a promise—

CAPO.

What to do?

ALTOUM

To make this edict: For a year and a day,
All royal suitors of her hand in marriage
Must answer first three riddles put by her:
To him who answers right she shall be wed;
But all who answer wrong shall straightway die
And their dissevered heads be spiked in scorn
High on the city's gate.

CAPO.

[*Looking at the gate*]

So those are they
Who answered wrong!

ALTOUM

None yet has answered right.

CAPO.

But why, my liege—

ALTOUM

Why did I give consent
To publish the mad edict? This is why:
I worship Turandot. There is no whim
Of hers I would not grant to make her happy,—
But ah!—how can I make her so?

CAPO.

Is she
Unhappy, then, in her success?

ALTOUM

At times
She weeps to hear the headsman's gong, but when
Her lovers cry to her for pity, straight
Her eyes grow cold with sudden cruelty
And give the sign for death.

CAPO.

Have you no clue
For this?

ALTOUM

[*Distractedly*]

No clue? Gods of my ancestors,
Have I not sought a thousand counsels, all
In vain!—A gentle girl, a dove of maidens,

Sudden transformed to be a thing of talons—
A harpy-tigress! Clue? What clue have I
For murder in the bosom of a dove?—

CAPO.

Softly, my liege. That is my specialty.

ALTOUM

So I have heard from specialists before;
Yet now I feel new hope. If you shall find
This clue—whether it be some hidden, strange
Indisposition, or some secret reason
Concealed by her—and *if you find the cure,*—
To you, and to these motley friends of yours,
I will bequeath power and provinces
And wealth unbounded. But—pay heed, Sir Capo!
If you shall *fail* to find this cause and cure,
By holy Confucius, I will *doom* you all
To tortures and slow death. So to perform
Your task, I grant one day—until the hour
Of noon to-morrow. Are you satisfied
To undertake the task? If not, begone!

CAPO.

Your majesty, I am most itching pleased
To undertake it—on conditions.

ALTOUM

What?

CAPO.

For this one day *I* must be emperor,
In place of you, and these my motley friends—
Prime-ministers.

ALTOUM

My star!—What then, Sir?

CAPO.

Then,
My liege, I most devoutly stake my head
And theirs, with these our masks thereto pertaining,
Not merely to ascertain the cause and cure
Of your fair daughter's malady, but also—
For this, my liege, is my *true* specialty!—
I undertake to see her happily
Plight in a perfect marriage of romance.

ALTOUM

Great Buddha! Now, this quickens my stale blood—
To meet one man of live audacity!
Ha! bid me abdicate—usurp my throne—
A one day's emperor!—Good; be it so.
Agreed:—But on your head the consequences!

CAPO.

May the consequences let my head be on!—
Where shall I find your daughter?

[*A deep bell sounds within the walls. Calaf reënters with Barak*]

ALTOUM

Hark! the gong!

CAPO.

What gong?

ALTOUM

The gong of death: the execution.
Another hapless lover has guessed wrong
The fateful riddles. Now the headsman holds
His head, and Turandot is coming here
In state, to impale the gory token—yonder.

BARAK

[*To Calaf*]

You hear!—You hear?

CALAF

O happy lover, whom
The dearest of women honors so in death!

BARAK

Madness!

ALTOUM

[*To Capocomico*]

By heaven, I am impatient of
Such slaughter. See you stop it.

CAPO.

[*Nodding loftily*]

We shall bear

In mind your supplication, Sir.——Meanwhile

My crown!

[*He extends his hand for Altoum's crown. Altoum, startled, smiles, takes it off and hands it to him*]

ALTOUM

Gods of my ancestors!

CAPO.

[*Putting on the crown*]

And now

Present to us our court!

ALTOUM

[*Bows, laughing*]

Well said, my liege!

[*Turning to the Chinese courtiers, he beckons them*]

Doctors and ministers of the royal Divan!
Witness our will:——Until to-morrow noon
We abdicate our throne, and in our place
Appoint, with all our high prerogatives,
Our friend and servant——Capocomico.
Salute your emperor!

CAPO.

[*Nodding affably*]

Emperor, *pro tem*!

THE CHINESE COURTIERS

[*With murmurs of astonishment, prostrate themselves before Capocomico*]

Salaam!

CAPO.

Not at all. Delighted! We will now

Present our friend and servant—Scaramouche,

Prime-Minister!

[*The courtiers salaam before Scaramouche, who puts his hand on his heart and blows them a kiss from his drawn sword-point*]

And next, Sir Harlequin,

Prime-Minister!

[*The courtiers repeat. Harlequin replies with a ballet-curtsy*]

His lordship, Pantaloon,

Prime-Minister!

[*The courtiers repeat. Pantaloon shuffles nervously*]

And Signore Punchinello,

Prime-Minister!

[*The courtiers repeat. Punchinello, tapping his nose, bows sagely. The four Maskers assume toploftical airs and gather about Capocomico*]

And now, Prime-Minister, are your four heads

All dumb? Your emperor awaits advice.

SCARAMOUCHE

By the belly of Baal, your majesty, I move

We all adjourn to breakfast.

PANTALOON

[*Quickly*]

Second the motion!

PUNCHINELLO

Hear! hear! Applause!

[*Harlequin dances to the gate*]

CAPO.

[*Correctively*]

No applause in court! The motion
Rests on the table—

[*To Scaramouche*]

with your breakfast.—Now
More pressing matters urge: Our imperial
Daughter—Princess of Pekin—comes.

ALTOUM

[*Gasping*]

Your daughter!

CAPO.

Daughter, *pro tem*!—

[*To all*]

The princess Turandot:
Salute her!

[*To the intermittent toll of the deep gong, soldiers enter with procession to slow, martial music. Amongst them, with regalia, a Headsman bears on a pike the head of a young man, which he places beside the others over the gate.*

Finally, accompanied by female slaves, comes Turandot, dressed like her followers in garb of gloomy splendor.

In the crowd Calaf gazes at her passionately. With him is Barak.

The Chinese courtiers prostrate themselves.

The Maskers bow in European fashion]

THE CHINESE COURTIERS AND CROWD

Turandot! Salaam!

CAPO.

[*Speaks familiarly to the emperor*]

Altoum,

Present to us our newly adopted daughter!

ALTOUM

Turandot, heaven to-day has interposed
To grant your prayers. Listen!

TURANDOT

[*Looking with wonder at Capocomico and the Maskers*]

I am listening, Sire.

ALTOUM

'Tis your strange prayer never to marry. Well,
Henceforth I vow no more to oppose your whim.
One year has passed and one day yet remains
Of my rash law that dooms your lovers to death.

[He points to the new head upon the wall]

For that one day, to celebrate my vow
And do you pleasure, I have appointed these
Princes of Faraway, to usher in
Our new régime. Sir Capocomico
Is now your emperor; these are your court
To make a festa of the law's last day.—
After to-morrow you are free forever.

TURANDOT

Sire, are you jesting?

CAPO.

Signorina, all
We dream or do is jesting, and ourselves
The butts of the jester. We are antics all.
To advertise it is my specialty.
Therefore, if we be kings or deuces hangs
On how the clever jester cuts his pack.
This cut I'm king, and

[Pointing to the Maskers]

red is trumps, not black.
So doff your mourning, daughter.

TURANDOT

If I am dreaming,
Or you are jesting, this is the pleasantest jest
My heart has dreamed in all one doleful year.

Princes of Faraway, I welcome you.
This bloody sport of spikèd lovers' heads—
I'm tired of playing it. Those heartless fools
That sought to wed a princess 'gainst her will—
Look how they read my riddle on the air!
Love is a slippery necklace.—Bring me laughter,
My one day's Sire, and I will bow me low
And kiss your garment.

CAPO.

Go and change your own, then,
To match our motley.

TURANDOT

I will go—and laugh
In going.

[*To her slaves*]

Come!

[*Turandot starts to return within the gate. Pushing through the crowd, Calaf prostrates himself before her, with a passionate cry*]

CALAF

Alms!—alms for hearts
That beg!

[*Reaching toward her, Calaf holds up the withered rose.*
Gazing, Turandot pauses an instant, moves past, but, looking back, staggers, trembling]

TURANDOT

Ah me!

[*Swaying, she swoons in the arms of her slave, Zelima*]

ZELIMA

My lady!

CAPO.

[*Rushing toward her, with Altoum*]

Quick! She's falling!

ALTOUM

Turandot!—Kill the beggar.

TURANDOT

[*Faintly, recovering*]

No, 'tis nothing.

[*To Capocomico*]

Here, give him this.

CAPO.

[*Taking it, astounded*]

Your ring?

TURANDOT

A token, Sire.—
A token of our new régime: to all
My people—blessing, and to beggars—love.

[*She goes out*]

ALTOUM

[*Going with her*]

Attend her well, Zelima.

[*All follow after, and at a gesture from Capocomico, pass out. Near the gate the Maskers pause and wait for Capocomico, who returns to Calaf*]

CAPO.

Fellow, rise!

[*Calaf staggers to his feet*]

Your most high princess graciously bestows
This alms—a ring, in token of her love
To all the world.

[*Taking it, Calaf falls again to the ground. Barak comes to him. Capocomico watches, and beckons, twinkling, to the Maskers*]

Now heaven witness this:—
He also swoons. My playboys, catch your cue.
Who said Romance is buried? Here is China
Where princesses and beggars swoon to meet!—

[*Surreptitiously, he takes from Calaf's side a wallet. Then beckons the Maskers.*]

Prime-Minister, follow your emperor!

[*He departs with the Maskers*]

BARAK

[*With solicitude*]

Calaf—my prince!

[*He raises him to a sitting posture*]

CALAF

[*Dazedly*]

Her ring!

BARAK

We must be gone gone—
Danger surrounds us here.

CALAF

[*Rising*]

Her ring for token!
But ah!—he said "to all the world."

BARAK

Be quick!

CALAF

[*With suddenness*]

I will. This instant I will follow her.

BARAK

Follow her!—what, to death?

CALAF

Death or delight,
Either or both, for death itself were joy
For her sake.

BARAK

Do you wear that ring in hope?

A beggar?

CALAF

No, she gave it as an alms,
"To all the world." The princess of the world
Would never stoop in love to wed with less
Than royal blood.—There is no hope for me,
A beggar.

BARAK

How, then—?

CALAF

I will go as prince—
As Calaf, prince of Astrakhan, I'll go
To guess her riddles—like those others.

BARAK

No!
That would be doubly death. Your head is forfeit
If you are even found.

CALAF

Few know me here, or none,
In Pekin; yet though every dog should know me
I'll do it.—Here, keep safe this beggar's cloak:
I love it for her sake. This ring and rose
Guard as your life. Come now; help me remove
This stain and straggled beard. Then wait for me,
Till I have won my love—or perish there!

[*Pointing to the heads on the gate, he rushes into the city.*]

BARAK

[*Following him*]

Lord of mad lovers, save him!

Curtain.

ACT SECOND

SCENE I: *A Room in the Harem*

On a low bench Zelima is seated, sewing a gorgeously embroidered garment. About her are other female slaves.

At the back stands Chang, the chief Eunuch.

ZELIMA

[*Stops sewing and listens*]

There! Hark! I hear it again.

CHANG

I can hear nothing.

ZELIMA

You're growing deaf, Chang. Some one is knocking—softly.

CHANG

[*Opening the door, left*]

No one is here.

ZELIMA

Below—at the outer door.

See who it is.

CHANG

I will see.

[*He goes out, closing the door. Zelima sews for a moment; then rises, puts away her needle and spreads out the garment, surveying it.*

From the right Turandot enters, splendidly arrayed.

She runs impetuously to Zelima and embraces her]

TURANDOT

Zelima! Zelima!
Little Zelima!

ZELIMA

[*Affectionately*]

My lady!

TURANDOT

Dance with me!—Dance!

ZELIMA

I heard a knocking, my lady.

TURANDOT

[*Pressing her left side*]

You heard it—here.
My lover is knocking, and I have let him in.

ZELIMA

[*Frightened*]

You've let him in, my lady?

TURANDOT

[*Laughing*]

Into my heart!
He came a-begging. Oh, does he love me, Zelima?

ZELIMA

[*Concernedly*]

He kept your rose.

TURANDOT

The rose I tossed from my garden
In Astrakhan, one year ago to-night—
Isn't he handsome, Zelima?

ZELIMA

[*With conscientious pause*]

Handsome, my lady?

TURANDOT

Splendid and fair like a prince!

ZELIMA

He is a beggar.

TURANDOT

I spoke of his soul—his eyes. His eyes are sapphires;
All other men's are clay.

ZELIMA

[*Dubiously*]

His face was dirty.

TURANDOT

[*Slapping Zelima's arm*]

Stop it, you dunce! His face was nobly tanned
By sun and rugged wind.

ZELIMA

I thought his beard—

TURANDOT

His beard—God did his best: I want no better.

ZELIMA

You—want a beard, my lady?

TURANDOT

Stupid Zelima!
Where's my new robe? I'll wear it to-day—for him.

ZELIMA

[*Helping her on with the embroidered garment*]

You like it?

TURANDOT

Are not gold and gorgeousness
For joy? To-morrow ends my year and a day.
Then no more suitors—no more severed heads!
I shall be free then—free to search for him
Through all the city.

ZELIMA

Search for a beggar! Why,
My lady?

TURANDOT

Must I scratch your silly eyes out
To make them see?—Of all men that love women,

I will have none for husband—if he'll have me—
But *him*, the man to whom I gave my ring.

ZELIMA

Holy Confucius save you, lady! You,
Princess of Pekin, wed a beggar!

TURANDOT

Hush!
Unless I dream so and rejoice to-day
Then I must wake and tear my flesh for grief
That I was born Princess of Pekin. Oh,
Little Zelima, let me dream I am
A beggar-maid, or he, my beggar—a prince!

ZELIMA

I hope your royal father hears no word
Of this, my lady. He would kill your lover
Sooner than you should wed him.

TURANDOT

I know it well.
So I have kept my secret this long year,
And let full many a brave prince lose his head
To hide my true love. Do not make me weep
Again for pity and despair. For now
Fresh hope has come. This Capocomico
Has changed my father's heart to set me free
To-morrow. Only one more day is left;
You only know my secret; none can guess it;
And for this final day there is no suitor

To claim my hand.

[*Chang enters, left, in perturbation. Turandot looks up inquiringly*]

Well—well?

CHANG

Another suitor
Has come, my lady.

TURANDOT

Nay, alas!

ZELIMA

What,—here?
Is he at the door?

CHANG

Not him,—the emperor
Is at the door. He comes to tell you, lady,
And asks admittance.

TURANDOT

What, my father!

CHANG

[*Fidgetting*]

Not
Your royal father: The new emperor
Is here.

TURANDOT

Sir Capo here!

ZELIMA

[*Appalled*]

Here, in the harem!

CHANG

What should I do, your highness?

TURANDOT

[*Staring*]

What can it mean?

CAPO.

[*Entering, left*]

The new régime, fair ladies!

[*To Zelima, who runs with the other slave girls toward the door, right*]

I beseech you,

Do not be timid: All true love romances

Are hatched in harems. 'Tis my specialty.

[*Dressed in robes of royal splendor, Capocomico stands smiling at them*]

TURANDOT

Sir, this intrusion breaks our ancient law.

CAPO.

To-day—O lovely daughter!—*I* am the law

And legalize intrusion.

[*To Chang*]

You may go.

[*Chang pauses, dubious, but at a gesture from Capo, departs hastily. Zelima goes timorously to Turandot, whose eyes flash*]

TURANDOT

Will you make entrance here against our wills,
Or why, then, have you come?

CAPO.

[*Smiling*]

For a beggar's sake.

TURANDOT

[*With sudden start*]

A beggar's?

CAPO.

What I bring will fill four ears—
No more.

TURANDOT

[*Faintly*]

Zelima, wait within—close by.

[*Zelima goes out, right with the slave girls*]

Well, Sire, what do you bring me?

CAPO.

Riches, child,
In a ragged wallet.

[*He takes out Calafs wallet, and holds it toward her.*]

TURANDOT

[*Starting*]

This! Why bring me this?

CAPO.

Hold it, and feel how heavy.

TURANDOT

[*Slowly takes it, peering in*]

Why, 'tis empty.

CAPO.

What is so heavy as an empty heart
Hollow with yearning! This has yearned for love
Until it cracked. Look there—those sorry gashes

TURANDOT

What should I do with it?

CAPO.

Heal its wounds, and fill it
With royal favor.

TURANDOT

[*Reticent*]

Sire, you talk in riddles.

CAPO.

Daughter, you kill in riddles.—Will you kill,
Or heal, this beggar's heart I bring?

TURANDOT

Ah me!

[*No longer suppressing her feelings, she kisses the wallet passionately.*]

How have you guessed my soul? How have you guessed?

CAPO.

The souls of lovers are my specialty.—
When princesses grow pale, and beggars swoon,
Then I bring forth my wallet—and prescribe.

TURANDOT

Alas—he swooned? Where is he? Is he ill?

CAPO.

Unnecessary questions, child: Of course
He swooned. Where is he? He's in love,
Of course, and so of course is deathly ill.

TURANDOT

Oh, by the simple truth you've torn from me,
Do not, I beg, speak sideling, but straight out:
That beggar whom I love—how fares he now?
Where have you left him?

CAPO.

By the city gate.
There, when he saw your ring, he fell in swoon;
And so I left him.

TURANDOT

[*Passionately*]

Find him! Find him for me,
And I will give you kingdoms!

CAPO.

Kingdoms, child,
Are shaky things. Give me your confidence:
Then I will find him for you.

TURANDOT

All my faith,
My gratitude and wonder—they are yours!—
When will you fetch him?

CAPO.

Soft! To achieve for you
Joy in a perfect marriage of romance—
That is *my* vow. 'Tis yours, for a single day,
To swear me loyalty.

TURANDOT

I swear it.—Ah,
But do not tell my father. He would kill
My hopes.

CAPO.

Your father—I will educate;
And for your low-born lover, I'll despatch
The eight proud legs of my prime-minister

To stalk the city till they stumble on him.

By nightfall, I will give you news what luck

They meet. Meantime, you must prepare once more

Your riddles for your final suitor.

TURANDOT

[*Appalled*]

What!

CAPO.

Keedur, the young khan of Beloochistan,

Waits in the hall below, to try his fate

To-day.

TURANDOT

Keedur? Another! Must another

Still die on this last day? Oh, misery!

And I to run the awful risk once more!—

When must this be?

CAPO.

This hour, in the great hall

Of the imperial Divan. Rest you merry,

My child, and whet your riddles sharp.—Good-bye!

TURANDOT

[*Detaining him by a swift gesture*]

Not yet! Stay yet a little: Help me!

CAPO.

How?

TURANDOT

To shape my riddles so no man that lives
Can answer them.

CAPO.

[*Bows, smiling*]
Why, that's my specialty.

TURANDOT

[*Slowly, with desperation.*]

Capo, those riddles hold his life or mine:
If Keedur guesses them—I'll kill myself.

Curtain

SCENE II: *Great Hall of the Emperor's Divan.*

On either side is a high tower, with entrance.

Down scene on the left stands the Emperor's throne, opposite the throne of Turandot.

As the curtain rises, Scaramouche, Punchinello, Pantaloon, and Harlequin enter, dragging in Barak by four purple ropes attached to his neck.

Barak carries a ragged bundle.

At the centre he falls, prostrating himself before them.

The four Maskers are dressed sumptuously in Chinese garments, worn over their own tattered garbs of motley, which—at times, when they gesticulate or move abruptly,—are fantastically visible.

BARAK

Mercy and clemency, your highnesses!

PUNCHINELLO

Your *highness*, slave! Address thy vermin speech

To the Prime-Minister.

BARAK

To which, O Lord?

SCARAMOUCHE

By the eye of Og and head of Hamongog,
To *us*, thou quaking mongrel! Howl thy prayers
Quadrately to thy quadrigeminal master!

BARAK

[*Revolving himself fearfully*]

Mercy, O Master!

PANTALOON

First confess thyself!
Where is he?

PUNCHINELLO

Where's thy fellow beggar? Speak!

SCARAMOUCHE

Tooth of the Turk!—Disgorge him!

[*Harlequin thwacks Barak on the head with his flat-stick*]

BARAK

Lord, I know not.
I am an old poor man. I have no fellow
To beg with me.

PANTALOON

Thou lousy bag of lies!

He swooned beside thee at the city gate.

PUNCHINELLO

He took the Princess' ring for alms. Where is he?

SCARAMOUCHE

[*Tightening his rope*]

By Sardanapalus! Squeeze off his neck

And pick the secret from his gullet.

BARAK

[*As Harlequin bangs him again*]

Spare me!

[*Enter, left, Capocomico*]

CAPO.

Hah! here's our beggar's crony.—Where's thy mate,

Old gaffer?

BARAK

Spare me, lord! I have no mate—

I beg alone.

CAPO.

Where was he found—this fellow?

SCARAMOUCHE

Godbodikins! We caught him gutter-skulking

Behind the palace.

CAPO.

What's here in this pack?

BARAK

[*Fearfully clutching his bundle*]

Old rags, your mightiness: poor worthless pickings.

CAPO.

Conduct him to my quarters. Search him there
And look what this contains.

[*The four begin to drag him out with the ropes*]

BARAK

A—yi! Alas!

PUNCHINELLO

[*Mocking him*]

A—yi, old pickings!

SCARAMOUCHE

[*Pulling*]

Sacrasacristan!
Heave-ho, my hearts!

CAPO.

Hold him in custody
Till I can question further.

BARAK

[*Crying aloud*]

Calaf, save me!

PANTALOON

We'll save 'ee in salt, old calf!

SCARAMOUCHE

Yank-ho, there!

[*They drag him out, left*]

CAPO.

[*Stands meditating*]

Calaf!

[*Hardly have they disappeared, when Calaf enters hastily, looking about him with a startled expression. He is dressed in princely regalia, and his face is shaved. Seeing Capo., he pauses abruptly, and makes obeisance*]

CAPO.

Greetings, Sir Keedur!—You are *searching* here?

CALAF

[*Embarrassed*]

Nothing, your majesty. It seemed I heard
A voice here cry in terror.

CAPO.

Cry—on *whom*?

CALAF

Nay, Sire, I do not know.

CAPO.

'Twas just a beggar
That cried at being expelled.

CALAF

Expelled?—Where to?

CAPO.

[*With a flitting smile*]

You—care to know?

CALAF

Nay, Sire, why should I care?

CAPO.

Nay, why indeed? You caught me querying.

CALAF

[*Turning to leave*]

Forgive that I disturbed your thoughts.

CAPO.

My thoughts
Were trying to construe the beggar's cry.
"Calaf, save me!" he called.

CALAF

[*Pausing, with a faint start*]

Ah—Calaf? So!

CAPO.

An odd coincidence, for 'tis one year
To-night since Calaf, prince of Astrakhan,
Perished by drowning in the river Yen.—

[*With slow emphasis*]

He was the Emperor's arch-enemy.

CALAF

[*Calmly*]

An odd coincidence!

CAPO.

And still more odd
It might be—might it not?—if Keedur, Khan
Of far Beloochistan, had chanced to know
Or meet this Calaf.

CALAF

Still more odd.

CAPO.

Perchance
He never did!

CALAF

[*Fidgetting slightly*]

I never met him, Sire.

CAPO.

[*With a quick glance*]

That being so, we must no more delay
Your audience with the princess. My ear itches.
Methinks by that your suit will prosper; let me
Conduct you to your place of waiting. Come,
And by the way, I will confide to you—
I have a specialty.

CALAF

In what, Sire?

CAPO.

[*Smiling, as they go out*]

Riddles.

[*Enter Altoum and Chang. They look after Capo as he departs*]

ALTOUM

In the harem, with my daughter—?

CHANG

[*Obsequiously*]

Even so,
O Majesty.

ALTOUM

And closeted, you say,
An hour with her!

CHANG

An hour, O Majesty.

ALTOUM

But you kept watch: The Princess, she was not
Alarmed?

CHANG

Her royal highness seemed
Moved in her spirit, O Majesty.

ALTOUM

Moved? So!
Well, Chang, inform me further what you note.
To-day this stranger reigns as Emperor.
Obey him.

[*Capo reënters, right*]

CHANG

[*Salaaming to a gesture of dismissal from Altoum*]

As your Majesty decrees.

[*Exit*]

ALTOUM

[*Greets Capo cordially*]

Hail, friend! You wear my Empire as you'd worn it
Life long.

CAPO.

[*Laughing*]

I'll wear it longer if you like.

ALTOUM

Perchance I'll let you. As for me, I feel
Lighthearted as a schoolboy playing truant.
This abdicating gives me appetite
For holidays.—And what success so far?

CAPO.

So far—perfection.

ALTOUM

Have you, then, discovered
My daughter's malady?

CAPO.

I've diagnosed
Already, and prescribed.

ALTOUM

[*Eagerly*]

What is the ailment?

CAPO.

Ah! question the doctor when he makes the cure.—
Another twenty hours!

ALTOUM

To rule is sweet,
I see. Good luck attend your reign! If so,
I have four kingdoms waiting for your fellows,

And for yourself a petty empire—*but*,

Forget not—Sire! For failure I've prepared

Five torture chambers and a sharpened axe.

CAPO.

To-morrow, then, four kingdoms shall have kings!

As for the petty empire, I'll return it

With compliments, and count myself well quit

To have served your Majesty and true Romance.

[*Kettledrums are sounded within*]

Now, then, to pass the first ordeal.—Pray follow!

ALTOUM

[*Attending him, left*]

This suitor Keedur—I like well his looks

And bearing. What if he should guess the riddles?

CAPO.

That lies now with the Fates—and they obey me.

[*They go out.*

To the sound of kettledrums, tambourines and music outside, the scene is now for a moment empty. Then from both entrances two processions enter simultaneously.

From the right enter Eunuchs and female slaves of the harem; from the left Chinese soldiers and courtiers of the Emperor's suite.

With ceremonial, salaaming and flare of music, the persons in the processions group themselves on either side about the thrones.

Entering last in their separate processions come Turandot and Capocomico—the latter accompanied by Altoum, as a subordinate.

On the right throne Turandot sits, on the left—Capocomico.

All the others prostrate themselves, except Altoum, who stands beside a lesser seat, at the right of Capo's throne.

Having taken their positions, at a signal from Capo, all are served with tea in little cups, which they sip simultaneously thrice, then resume their former obeisances.

To this gathering now enter three of the Maskers—Scaramouche, Punchinello and Pantaloon—bearing severally three golden platters, on which stand little jeweled boxes, closed.

Behind them follows Harlequin, who bears a great parchment roll, which—with bows and ballet-dancings—he lays before the throne of Capo; then takes his stand at Capo's left.

Lastly Calaf enters, alone.

Bowing to the throne, he remains in the centre, where he gazes rapt at Turandot.

Capo now rises, and Altoum seats himself]

CAPO.

Powers of our royal Divan and our Harem,

Once more, in token of our sovereign will,

We are assembled. Let the law be read!

[*He sits. Harlequin, stepping forward with a flourish, presents the roll of parchment to Punchinello, who, exchanging with him his platter for the script, reads in a shrill voice*]

PUNCHINELLO

To high Confucius and our ancestors—

Worship and awe! The edict of Altoum

In re the royal princess Turandot

Perpends: To suitors of her august hand

Who guess her riddles—marriage, riches, joy!

To all who fail—shame, execution, death!

None save of royal blood shall qualify.

[*Harlequin receives back the roll from Punchinello, and resumes his place*]

CAPO.

Who seeks the august hand of Turandot?

CALAF

[*Standing forward*]

I, Keedur, Khan of great Beloochistan.

CAPO.

Keedur, full many noble youths before you
Have made this trial; all have failed—and died.
Have you considered well their doom, O Khan?

CALAF

There is no doom for me but loss of her;
If then I fail, death can but ease my doom.

TURANDOT

[*In a low voice*]

His eyes, Zelima! Oh, I would he'd look
Another way.

ZELIMA

It is a lovely youth.

CAPO.

Think well, you are young. You may even still withdraw
And live these many years.

CALAF

[*His eyes meeting Turandot's, who looks at him anxiously*]

If I must die,
I shall have lived forever in this instant.

CAPO.

Then let the trial proceed.

TURANDOT

Fair stranger, first
Hear me, and so relent.

CALAF

My spirit, lady,
Stands tiptoe to your words.

TURANDOT

You have not well
Considered what you seek; but I, who know,
Can better advise you. Turandot you seek,
But I, who know this Turandot, can tell you
She is a lady of too little worth
To cause the noble lineage in your blood
To die. She neither wants you, nor your death.
Now leave her, Sir, and give her leave to wish you
Joy of your twice escape.

CALAF

I hear you, yet
I hear like one who dies out on the desert
And dreams he hears sweet water tinkling.—Lady,
I parch and drink dream-water. Would you dash
That boon from my soul's lips?

TURANDOT

Nay, then, no more!

Hear now my riddles.—But, I pray you, look not
This way, but elsewhere.

CALAF

I will close my eyes
And look upon you, listening.—I am ready.

[*Closing his eyes, he waits with a faint smile*]

TURANDOT

Tell me, O friend: What is that flower
Which, dying, steals its lover's breath,
And being dead, still blooms in death,
Living beyond its little hour
To grow more sweet in fragrance as it grows
In memory?

[*Turandot gazes pityingly. Calaf speaks with closed eyes*]

CALAF

A withered rose.

[*Turandot starts suddenly from her throne and sinks back, whispering to Zelima. Capo despatches Harlequin to Turandot, who gives him tremblingly a key, which he carries to Scaramouche*]

CAPO.

Unlock the secret box.

SCARAMOUCHE

[*As Harlequin unlocks the little box on his platter and presents to him a strip of parchment from within it, reads aloud*]

A withered rose.

[A murmur runs through the assembly]

ALTOUM

Now by my star, well guessed!

CAPO.

[With a gesture for silence]

The second riddle!

TURANDOT

[With emotion]

Stranger, you are the first of all my suitors
That ever reached the second.—I have spoken
To you in pity, but my pity now
Is for myself, lest you should guess too well.
Cease, then, I beg you. Rest content with passing
Your rivals. Go! And I will give you triumph
In your departure.

ALTOUM

Shame! Fair play, my daughter!

CAPO.

Silence, my lord Altoum!—What says the Khan?

CALAF

I answer here by law, risking my death.
Therefore, O lady, since my love of you
Surpasses life, I claim my right of law.

TURANDOT

[*Her eyes flashing*]

By heaven, cold prince, I see I wasted pity
Upon a heart of ice. Meet, then, your fate!
I will not weep to watch the headsman's axe.

CALAF

I trust you will not, princess.—I am ready.

TURANDOT

[*To Zelima*]

O fiend! My fingers itch to scratch him.

[*To Calaf*]

Hear, then:
Reveal, O youth: What is that fetter
Which, chaining, sets its captive free,
But broken, makes of liberty
A weary bondage, little better
Than death, to one whose spirits mount and sing
In manacles?

[*Calaf remains silent, pressing his closed eyes in thought. Altoum leans forward. The people mutter low. Turandot gazes disdainfully. Soon, letting his raised hands fall, Calaf speaks with tense calmness.*]

CALAF

A lover's ring.

TURANDOT

[*Cries out*]

What's that?

[*Clutching Zelima's arm*]

My God! here is some treachery.

CAPO.

Open the second lock!

[*Harlequin unlocks the little box held by Punchinello, who reads aloud*]

PUNCHINELLO

A lover's ring.

[*A great murmur goes up from the assembly*]

ALTOUM

Wondrous! The fates are with him.

TURANDOT

[*Rising, fiercely*]

Not the fates fates—
The fiends are with him. I cry out upon
This answer. Some perfidious hand
Has tampered with those locks.

CAPO.

Respect this hall
And presence, Princess: *We* shall judge alone.

TURANDOT

False friend, is this your pay for all my trust,
And this the perfect joy you bid me hope for?

[*To Altoum*]

Father, I cry on you to right this wrong!

ALTOUM

The wrong is yours to flout your own decree.
But right or wrong, my power is hushed: Not here
But yonder sits the Emperor of China.

TURANDOT

Why, this is monstrous. I am sold a slave
By an abdicated father and a motley
Who apes the emperor in a player's mask!—
I'll put no further riddle.

CAPO.

[*Smiling*]

As you like,
Princess, but let us keep our humors. If
There be no final riddle, Keedur wins:
The priests are ready to perform your wedding.

TURANDOT

[*Trembling with rage*]

My wedding!—Ah, then, I am duped indeed,
And must submit to treachery. But you—
O subtle Khan, dream not to shame me so,
And win. I will not *live* to be your wife.—
Do you still claim your riddle?

CALAF

[*Who has stood in utter calmness*]

I am ready.

TURANDOT

[*In fury*]

Then may your answer spike your head in death!

[*Clutching her throne, she speaks with voice quivering*]

Reply, O Prince: What may that be
Which, light of heart, causes despite,
But heavy-laden, renders light

Its bearer, making care so free
That kings might give their crowns to call it
Their treasure house?

[*A deep hush falls on the assembly. Calaf stands, silent, swaying.*
Slowly he totters and falls on the steps of Capo's Throne.
There, as Harlequin raises him, Capo whispers swiftly at his ear. Suddenly then, fixing
his eyes on Turandot, who stands pale and rigid, Calaf speaks thrillingly.]

CALAF

A beggar's wallet.

TURANDOT

[*With a low cry, holding her side*]

Ah!

CAPO.

[*To Harlequin*]

Quickly!—The third key!

[*Swiftly Harlequin unlocks the box held by Pantaloon, who reads aloud*]

A beggar's wallet.

TURANDOT

[*Turning, desperately*]

Zelima!

ZELIMA

[*Screaming*]

Lady!

[*Snatching from Zelima a little dagger, she lifts it and strikes at her own breast. Leaping to the throne, Calaf intercepts her and turns the dagger against himself*]

CALAF

Not you, my love!

CAPO.

Disarm them!

ALTOUM

Turandot!

[*Amid uproar, the four Maskers rush upon Calaf and wrest from him the dagger*]

TURANDOT

[*With fierce disdain*]

Coward hearts!

CALAF

[*Uplifting his hands to Capo*]

Sire, hear my plea!

CAPO.

Order and silence!—Speak, Sir Keedur.

CALAF

Sire,
If I have won this ordeal by the law—
Declare it.

CAPO.

You have won.

CALAF

Then I renounce
All I have won, and place before this court
A counter plea. Shall it be granted?

CAPO.

What
Do you petition?

CALAF

Sire, since it would shame me
And her, to take this noble princess' hand
Without her heart, I quit my claim, but ask
In substitute, a boon:—I, whom you call
Sir Keedur, Khan, am royal and a prince,
But I am not Khan of Beloochistan.
Keedur is not my name.

TURANDOT

So, treachery
Once more!

ALTOUM

Peace, daughter!

CAPO.

[*To Calaf*]

Speak. What is your plea?

CALAF

This, Sire: Since I have answered now three riddles
Of Turandot, that she—to make fair play—
Shall answer one of mine. If she shall guess it,
I then depart, but if she fail, I stay—
And wed her.

TURANDOT

[*Scornfully to Capo*]

Ha! This jesting, Sire, fits well
Your new régime.

CAPO.

[*To Calaf*]

What is your riddle?

CALAF

This:
Reveal, O Lady: What is he,

His true-born name,

His father's fame,

Who, desperate for love of thee,

Assumed from far Beloochistan

The false name—Keedur, Khan?

TURANDOT

Nay sir, I'd scorn to answer. What you are,
Or who, or whence—to me henceforth 'tis nothing.

CAPO.

Softly, quick tongue! To us the game seems fair.
Sir nameless lover, you shall have your plea.
'Tis granted.

TURANDOT

[*Trembling with rage*]

What!—O miracle of shame!
Perfidious Masker!

CAPO.

This your riddle shall
Be answered here to-morrow by this lady,
Or else you shall be wedded to her here
Before high noon.

TURANDOT

[*Descending swiftly from the throne*]

Fools! I defy you—both!

[*Flinging her sceptre at Capo's feet, she rushes out*]

CAPO.

[*Rising*]

Follow her!

[*At his gesture, the four Maskers follow after. Amid loud murmur and commotion Calaf stands staring at the empty throne*]

Curtain

ACT THIRD

SCENE I: *An anteroom in the harem. Night.*

In the centre of the columned room is a table, on which—softly illumined—stands a large crystal bowl, filled with swimming gold fishes.

Nearby, Turandot sits weeping, Zelima beside her. Outside, the shrill voice of Punchinello is heard singing to the twang of stringed instruments:

O Lady, Lady, let fall your tears

No more, no more, for foolish fears,

But let in your true playfellow;

For Sorrow's a thief

Brings Love to grief,

But a merry heart makes him mellow,

And a merry heart, O, a merry heart

Never yet kept fond lovers apart,

Nor pinched the shoe of their Punchinello.

TURANDOT

[*Savagely*]

Drive them away, Zelima! Drive them away!

PUNCHINELLO, SCARAMOUCHE, AND PANTALOON

[*Singing together outside*]

And a merry heart, O, a merry heart

Never yet kept fond lovers apart!

ZELIMA

[*Going to the door, puts her head out*]

Begone!

[*She returns to Turandot. The twanging outside decreases, but still continues*]

Take courage, Lady.

TURANDOT

Oh, I have lost
Courage and faith and kindness. All is dark—
Dark and disgrace.

ZELIMA

'Tis no disgrace to win
A husband.

TURANDOT

Win him!—To be tricked and sold
In slavery to one I love not—lose
The one I love, and truckle to the word
Of an upstart—a false, masquing popinjay
Of an emperor!—Yet, no disgrace! Ah me,
Why did your little dagger fail me? Now
I have no pluck of soul to try once more.

ZELIMA

The gods forbid! 'Twere very wicked, Lady:
And him, that saved you, and gave back your freedom
So gentlemanly!

TURANDOT

Ha! and caught me again
With his own riddle! Heaven, I hate him. Yet—
Zelima, did you see his eyes?

ZELIMA

[*Nodding*]

Most strangelike
They were.

TURANDOT

I must not think upon his eyes,
Or I might hate him less. No, only one
Of all men wears the gazes which I love,
And he is lost to me.

ZELIMA

Why lost, my Lady?
The emperor promised you to search the city
And find your beggar.

TURANDOT

Capo's promises
Are like himself—all lies. Nay, I must answer
This false Khan's riddle, or be doomed to-morrow.
But how?—"His true-born name, his father's fame—"
Where shall I find the clue? Ah, heartless fate
And stony hearted men!

THE VOICE OF PUNCHINELLO

[*Sings outside to the instruments*]

O Lady, Lady, lift up your moan
No more, no more 'gainst hearts of stone,
But let in your blithe playfellow!

TURANDOT

[*Wildly*]

Go! Stop them!

THE VOICE OF PUNCHINELLO

For a stubborn will
Makes Love to be ill,
But a merry heart makes him well, O!
And a merry heart—

ZELIMA

[*Opening the door*]

Stop
Your noises!

PUNCHINELLO

[*Outside*]

—O, a merry heart
Never yet kept fond lovers apart,
Nor tweaked the nose of their Punchinello.

ZELIMA

Cease! Her royal highness orders—

PUNCHINELLO, SCARAMOUCHE AND PANTALOON

[*Pushing past Zelima, enter the room bearing bright Chinese lanterns, and singing in chorus*]

A merry heart, O, a merry heart
Never yet kept fond lovers apart!

[Joined by Harlequin, they pause together before Turandot and, pointing simultaneously their left toes, strike sharply their instruments with a sweeping bow]

TURANDOT

What fresh presumption of your brazen lord
Is this?

PUNCHINELLO

This is our homage, Lady, Lady!

[Thrumming their instruments again,
they accompany a dance of Harlequin,
who by his pantomime indicates
to Turandot the bowl of gold fishes,
while Punchinello lilts shrilly:]

And thus our Harlequin: He's showing
How all our hearts be overflowing
With little, lovely, golden wishes
For your delight—as fine as fishes!

TURANDOT

Go—go!

[Harlequin draws back]

Why have you come?

PUNCHINELLO

To celebrate
Our lord Sir Capo's great discovery.

PANTALOON

[Mysteriously]

He's found.

TURANDOT

Who's found?

SCARAMOUCHE

[*Darkly*]

By the yawn of Jonah's whale,
We have disbellied him from Pekin's maw
And blackest hollowness.

PUNCHINELLO

He's trapped, my Lady!

TURANDOT

[*Chafing*]

Will you tell *who*?

PUNCHINELLO

[*In a loud whisper*]

The beggar.

SCARAMOUCHE AND PANTALOON

[*Sepulchrally*]

Hush!

TURANDOT

[*Faintly*]

A beggar!

SCARAMOUCHE

[*Speaks at her ear*]

The louse-gray mongrel with the chalkish beard—
We've got him kennelled, ha!

TURANDOT

An *old* man?

PANTALOON

[*Nodding*]

Pickled!

TURANDOT

Alas! What are these tidings? Have you searched
Only to find an old poor man?

CAPO.

[*Who has entered behind them*]

They found
Your beggar's gaffer, Lady.—Barak he
Is called, and lies imprisoned now below,
Where I will learn from him about your lover.

TURANDOT

[*Bitterly*]

So *you* come too. Have you, then, come to break
Once more the vow you made?

CAPO.

[*Quietly*]

A single day,

Lady, you swore me faith and loyalty;

Yet in one little hour you cast away

Your faith, to call me traitor.

TURANDOT

Had I cause,

Or no?

CAPO.

Is there good cause to break an oath?

TURANDOT

You broke your own. You vowed to achieve for me

Joy—joy, and perfect marriage with my love.—

Am I, then, joyful? Am I with my love?

CAPO.

A single day; a single day, I said!

TURANDOT

So by to-morrow I must wed this Khan,

This nameless prince—unless I guess his name.

CAPO.

Why not, then, guess it?

TURANDOT

[*Glancing quickly*]

How?

CAPO.

[*Indulgently*]

Will you renew

Your broken allegiance?

TURANDOT

I am desperate.

I will do anything to free myself.—

What shall I do?

CAPO.

First swear me faith again.

TURANDOT

I swear it. Now tell!

CAPO.

How easily ladies swear

When they are in love!—Prime-Minister, retire!

[*The four Maskers, bowing, withdraw to the background, where they are entertained by Zelima, whom they instruct to play upon their instruments with a low strumming*]

In the general practice of my specialties,

Lady, I often recommend for love

A sleeping-charm—like this.

[*Capo takes from his sleeve a small vial and hands it to Turandot*]

TURANDOT

What should I do

With this?

CAPO.

This, if 'tis poured upon the sleeping lips
Of man by a maid, or maiden by a man,
Will make the sleeper murmur in his dream
Whatever secret thing his soul conceals
When it is asked of him.

TURANDOT

[*After a pause, gives a sudden cry of joy*]

Ah, now I see!—
But how can I find access to this Khan
When he is sleeping?

CAPO.

I am emperor,
And by my new régime, at midnight, all
The guards retire, and in the men's hall, men
May pass unnoticed by the others.

TURANDOT

[*Searchingly*]

Men?

CAPO.

[*Calls, beckoning*]

Here, Harlequin!—I pray you, princess, stand
Back to back with this boy.

[*Turandot looks puzzled, and then turns and stands back to back with Harlequin. Capo measures their heights with his flattened hand. They separate and Capo indicates Harlequin*]

A hair's breadth higher.

[*With a questioning glance at Turandot*]

A hair's breadth! Will you risk it—by a hair?

TURANDOT

[*Growing suddenly radiant*]

O wonderful!—At midnight, did you say?

CAPO.

[*Smiling*]

Now are we friends—and may I kiss your hand?

TURANDOT

[*Ardently*]

No, I will kiss yours!

[*She seizes Capo's hand and kisses it. He laughs softly*]

Curtain

SCENE II: *A bedchamber, mysteriously lighted. The room is vast and magnificent. In the centre, by a divan couch, Calaf is seated in deep brooding.*

CALAF

If she should guess!—If she should fail to guess!
If she should fail to guess!—If she should guess!
O endless, awful night, you are like thought—
Hollow, unanswering and full of echoes!
And like my heart you, too, are sleepless, yearning
With dim and palpitating mystery.

If she should guess?—Then would I doubly lose
My love—my life. If she should fail to guess?
Then how might I dare hold her to my bond
And wed against her will?—If she should guess—
If she should fail—Ah, God! The night gives back
Only my emptiness, and moment builds
On moment mountains of hell, and here I sit
Alone.

[*Rising, he reaches his arms with a low cry*]

Alone!

CAPO.

[*Entering in the dimness*]

There is no loneliness
Where thoughts are merry.

CALAF

[*Staring at him for a moment*]

Merry!—Sire, I have
Forgot the meaning of that word.

CAPO.

Recall it,
Then, quickly, for I bring you pleasant news.

CALAF

[*Eagerly*]

From her? from *her*, O Sire?

CAPO.

From Turandot.
The lady loves you.

CALAF

Loves me! You are mad,
Or jesting.

CAPO.

To the sober-serious
Jesting's a sort of madness.—But no matter.
The lady loves you none the less.

CALAF

How is it
Possible?

CAPO.

You've forgot my specialty
So soon?—or am I skilled in guessing riddles?

CALAF

I should have failed without you.

CAPO.

Will you try me
Again?

CALAF

But how—

CAPO.

Come hither in more light.

[*Calaf moves out of the deeper shadow. Capo tips Calaf's face upwards, examining it*]

What color are your eyes?

CALAF

I do not know.

CAPO.

[*Nods approvingly*]

Sapphire.—That might describe them, with some license
Of love and rhetoric.

CALAF

What have my eyes
To do with guessing riddles?

CAPO.

Much to do!
They have to close and go to sleep, before
The guessing. Softly now: lie down and close them
Until to-morrow.

CALAF

Would I might!

CAPO.

Then do so!
For on to-morrow morn, I promise you
Delight—and perfect marriage with your love.

CALAF

O friend, I am too weary to refuse.

I will lie down and dream it is to-morrow.

[*He lies on the couch. A far chiming is heard*]

What bell is sounding?

CAPO.

Midnight.—Merry dreams!

[*Capo steals out. Calaf closes his eyes and is still. The room is silent and dim. After a few moments, out of the darkness there emerges, scarlet and pied, the Figure of Harlequin, who tiptoes toward the couch. At a sigh from Calaf, the Figure starts back, returning more reticently. Again Calaf murmurs in his sleep:*]

CALAF

Turandot! Lady beloved!

[*Standing in a shaft of vague light, the Figure of Harlequin lifts cautiously a vial and, unstopping it, dances softly three times around the divan; then pauses close to Calaf, who murmurs once more*]

Princess! Love.

THE FIGURE OF HARLEQUIN

[*Chants in a low voice*]

Reveal, O dreamer: What is he,

His true-born name,

His father's fame,

Who, desperate for love of me,

Assumed from far Beloochistan

The false name—Keedur, Khan!

[*Bending above the dreaming form of Calaf, the Figure sprinkles from the vial upon his lips; then draws back and listens*]

CALAF

[*Murmurs louder in his sleep*]

Be gracious unto me: Calaf, the son
Of Timur, King of Astrakhan!

THE FIGURE OF HARLEQUIN

[*Laughing silverly*]

Aha!
Calaf! Calaf, the son of Timur, King
Of Astrakhan!

CALAF

[*Starting up on the divan*]

Who calls me?

THE FIGURE

[*Lifting a mandolin strung from the shoulder, strikes a swift chord and bounds away toward the door*]

Ahaha!

CALAF

[*Leaping to the floor, and following*]

What are you? Stop!

[*The Figure pauses*]

Come from your shadow!

[*The Figure takes a timid step forward, and stops*]

You!
You, the dumb player, servant of our lord

The emperor! What brings you here?

THE FIGURE

Aha!
Reveal, O Lady: What is he
His true-born name,
His father's fame—

CALAF

How's that? Can the dumb speak?

THE FIGURE

Calaf, the son
Of Timur—hail!

CALAF

By heaven, a spy!

[*He springs toward the door. The Figure tries to pass him but, thwarted, leaps back*]

Not yet!
You shall not go till I have plucked the face
Out of that mask.

[*At the door he turns the key and takes it*]

The door is locked. Reveal
Yourself!

[*The Figure draws away. He strides toward it. It escapes*]

Light footed imp! Now by my soul,
You shall not live to blab beyond these walls
The secret you have stolen from my sleep.

[He starts again toward the Figure. It dances away from him, striking the strings of its mandolin. Round the great couch and about the shadowy room he pursues it, ever eluding him. Suddenly he pauses, and stares]

Stay! Am I, then, asleep? Are you indeed

Some imp of dreamland, sent to plague my soul

With fever shuttle-dances, a pied phantom

Painting the dark, and tinkling with your timbrel

These rafters of my riddle-tortured brain?—

If she should guess—If she should fail to guess!—

O Night, it is your Echo, mocking me:

'Tis but a Question, and beneath that mask

There are no lips to answer!

[Desperately, he throws himself down by the couch, burying his face against it. After a moment, the Figure approaches, cautious, surveys his prone form closely, bends as if to snatch at his robe, but draws back and stands hesitant; then with a gesture half frightened removes its mask, and speaks low]

THE FIGURE

Calaf, son

Of Timur—grace! Give me the key!

[Turning, Calaf slowly staggers to his feet, gazing with awe on the face of Turandot]

CALAF

O Dream!

Dream of my love transmuted to a boy—

O little dream in motley, speak once more!

TURANDOT

The key! Unlock the door, and let me forth.

CALAF

My lady—and her voice! Yet, shining boy,
Before my soul loses belief in you,
Still let me wonder, looking on your image,
And worship at your shrine—Saint Harlequin!

[*He kneels before her*]

TURANDOT

I do not ask for worship—but a key.

CALAF

The key you ask for locks the gate of heaven
And we are shut within. Love builds him bars
To stablish heaven where lovers are locked in.

TURANDOT

Lovers? You dare much.

CALAF

[*Rising*]

He dared more, to say
You love me, and I dared believe.

TURANDOT

[*Amazed*]

Who dared
To say it?

CALAF

He who shuttles through our lives,

Unriddling and riddling, like a restless loom—
The motley emperor.

TURANDOT

Capocomico!
He is a jester, Sir.

CALAF

Did he, then, jest
To furnish you that vial in your hand
And charm the fateful secret from my lips
Into your power? Ah, if you do not love me,
Why have you stolen here now to drag my name
From dreams—Calaf, your father's enemy,
Doomed unto death?

TURANDOT

[*Struggling with herself*]

Nay, ask not.

CALAF

Turandot,
Princess of Pekin, stoops not to betray
Her enemy, nor steal a riddle's answer
Thiefwise by night, to slay her enemy.
The thought is slander. No!—Therefore you love me:
So you have robbed—to save me.

TURANDOT

Turn your eyes
Away!

CALAF

Is it not so, Lady beloved?

TURANDOT

Oh, ask not with your eyes!—Nor with your thoughts
Ask not why this bold Harlequin is here
Thiefwise by night, to steal your secret name;
But let me go!

CALAF

[*Holding out the key, gazes at her*]

Will you, then, go?

TURANDOT

[*Reaches for it, but pauses and turns back her hand, screening her face*]

Your eyes!
They blind the space between. I cannot grope
The key I reach for.

CALAF

Will you go?

TURANDOT

The air
Is dim, but bright with pathways to your face,
And where they lead I falter, like a moth
To where the lamp shines.

CALAF

[*In hushed triumph*]

You will stay!

TURANDOT

O dark!
What light and darkness and the murmur of waters
Lure me toward you?

CALAF

Night and yearning stars
And rush of winds blend us, beloved. Listen!
Look in my eyes, O love!—Lean to my lips!

TURANDOT

[*Closing her eyes*]

I lean: Let me not fall!

CALAF

Thus will I save you!

[*Reaching his arms passionately, he kisses her*]

TURANDOT

[*Starting back, with a cry*]

Ah me! I am betrayed.

CALAF

By Buddha, I swear—

TURANDOT

Destroyed. O shame of all my vows forsworn,
Where have I fallen?

CALAF

On your lover's heart.

Look, it is I.

TURANDOT

Who's there?

CALAF

Calaf, your prince.

TURANDOT

Calaf!—Now shame put acid on my lips

And sere them of your kiss! A prince hath touched me!

O you poor bloody heads on Pekin's wall,

Have you, then, died for this?—and Turandot

Shamed by a prince at last!

CALAF

Lady, I beg—

TURANDOT

Not that!—Ah, do not stab me with that word,

And make me bleed for one who *begs*.—The key,

Give me the key!

CALAF

Mistress, your words go by me

Like leaves blown wildly. I cannot gather them.

TURANDOT

Sir prince, I blow them wildly, and I care not

Whither they whirl.

CALAF

Love changes blood to wine.
The kiss of our communion hath turned wine
To madden you.

TURANDOT

The key!

CALAF

[*Giving her the key*]

Take it, my lady,
So you may know your freedom and my love,
And me your lover, Calaf.

TURANDOT

Calaf, not
My lover.—Calaf, or Keedur, Khan, you are
Mine enemy in my power.—Until to-morrow,
Good-night!

[*She hastens toward the door. Grasping her arm, his eyes glow passionately*]

CALAF

You came here to betray me?—Speak!

TURANDOT

I came to win your secret, and to shame you
To-morrow at the trial. Let me pass.

CALAF

No! We are in each other's power. Let doom
Strike on us both together.

[*Inexorably he compels her. She sinks on the couch*]

TURANDOT

In your power!
What, I? You would not dare—

CALAF

Who would not dare?
Infinite ages climbed to this little moment;
Infinite ages shall sink after it.
I stand here on its peak to make it mine.—
Open the door!

TURANDOT

[*Trembling*]

Open it?—What will you do?

CALAF

Now shall the rafters of your palace ring
With "Turandot, the Harlequin, Calaf's lover
Stolen to his arms beside his midnight couch!"

TURANDOT

[*Shrinking from his gesture*]

Touch me not!

CALAF

[*Seizing her*]

Wine! Your kiss turns in my blood
To wine of fire poured foaming, and the flames
Burn outward toward your lips.

TURANDOT

Kiss not again!
Be merciful, and hear me!

CALAF

Mercy cries
To God, not to our enemy.—Your lips!

TURANDOT

[*With fearful appeal*]

My lover, then!

CALAF

[*Drawing back amazed*]

Your lover!

TURANDOT

Yea—my love!
Your eyes—*another* blazes in your eyes.

CALAF

Another! Who?

TURANDOT

The noblest in this world:

I love him. I have sworn it. Yet—O Yet—

My flesh cries out to yours, my soul to yours,

My lips, my lips to yours.

CALAF

[*Clasping her*]

Ha, mine at last!

TURANDOT

[*Repulsing him*]

Clasp me not, lest I cling to you.—No more!

I *will* not. I am his. No kiss of yours

Can quench his burning image. Let me go!

But ah, the spell and rapture of your arms—

Reach them where yearning lovers starve in hell,

And bless them.—Stop! My body and soul are *his*.

I hate you—I hate you—hate you!

[*She rushes into the dark. Calaf reaches—groping—with a wild cry.*]

Curtain

ACT FOURTH

The scene is the same as the second act, scene second, except that the back of the great hall of the emperor's Divan is now hidden by a decorated curtain. The assembly is gathered as before: Capocomico, Turandot and Altoum seated on their larger and lesser thrones.

Before them, Harlequin, Scaramouche, Punchinello and Pantaloon are performing a dance.

At its conclusion Capocomico rises, and addresses the Maskers.

CAPOCOMICO

Enough! Go, bring the nameless prince before us.

[Dismissing them with a gesture, he turns toward Altoum]

Altoum,—our greater emperor, the Sun,

Sits higher even than our august selves,

And soon shall set his throne at highest noon.

Then must I abdicate my one day's reign,

First having sealed your daughter's perfect marriage,

Ending in joy her doleful year and a day.

Therefore, in those brief minutes which are left me

To consummate these little things, I pray you

Deign of your courtesy to take my seat

And let me do the honors.

ALTOUM

[Rising from his lesser place]

As you will!

Till noon, my thanks for hospitality.

CAPO.

Oh, not at all!

[Pointing to his seat]

Pray, make yourself at home.

[*As they pass each other to change places, Altoum speaks to Capo in lower voice*]

Have you performed your task, and saved your head?

CAPO.

My head was never more attached to me.

TURANDOT

[*Bending from her throne*]

A word, my liege?

CAPO.

Nay, but a hundred, lady!

[*He goes to her side. She speaks to him low*]

TURANDOT

Have you kept faith with me? Ah—is he found—
My heart's desire?

CAPO.

Your heart's desire is found,
And waits for you.

TURANDOT

[*Excitedly*]

Where is he?

CAPO.

Lo, he comes!

[*Pointing toward the entrance, he goes to the lesser throne. With music of their stringed instruments, the four Maskers usher in Calaf, haggard and dishevelled. Turandot starts, with a cry and look of bewilderment at Capo. Capo addresses Altoum and the Divan*]

Your Majesty and lords, the nameless prince

Awaits to learn his name from Turandot.

CALAF

[*Stepping forward fiercely*]

He waits not, for his name has been betrayed

To her—and you, false jester, have betrayed it.

ALTOUM

[*Amid commotion*]

What's that?

CALAF

My liege, why should I play the fool

In a Masker's comedy? Death holds less scorn

Than being duped to dance in a puppet-show

To tinkling mandolins.

ALTOUM

Speak out your grievance!

CALAF

I stand here in your power, and his.—At midnight,

By secret sprinkling of a sleeping-charm,

This masker sent to rob my dreaming lips

Of the answer to my riddle—

ALTOUM

Gods! to rob?

Your proofs of this!

CALAF

The proofs stand up in me.

I who did deem it heaven to love your daughter

Have proved it hell. Your daughter knows my secret,

And all the ravage hidden in my name,

Yet am I nothing, my damnation—nothing

To her, who loves another.

ALTOUM

[*Startled*]

What—other? Who?

CALAF

"The noblest in the world."—O noble world,

There aspiration earns its crown of scorn,

And baseness wins nobility! In such,

I'd liever be a beggar. But enough!

My fate indeed is nothing, and my name—

My name is—

TURANDOT

Stop! your riddle goes unanswered.

Go you in peace—and friendship. You, Sir Capo,

Who keep your faith so strangely, set before me

The heart of my desire.

CAPO.

He stands before you.

TURANDOT

Trick me not also. Keep your promise still.
This man is Calaf, Son of Timur, not
My heart's desire.

ALTOUM

[*Rising, wrathful*]

How! Calaf, Son of Timur!

CALAF

Not drowned my liege, in water—but in grief.

ALTOUM

My darkest enemy.—So, Capo, this
Is he whom you would wed within my house
To my own daughter—Prince of Astrakhan!
Now by my star, the doom upon his head
Shall fall on yours—and doubly. I, it seems,
I, too, am duped!

TURANDOT

[*Brokenly*]

He has betrayed us all.

CAPO.

A single day is short to make all snug.
The Lord took six.

ALTOUM

A single day is all
My word allowed. I see! You bungled, fool,
Striving to save your neck, but now your time
Hangs at the stroke, and you have failed me. Doom
Falls on you and your fellows!

THE MASKERS

[*Trying unsuccessfully to salaam*]

Mercy, Sire!

CAPO.

[*Behind his hand chiding them*]

Where are your manners, my Prime-minister?
Venetian bows are still the mode in court,
Whilst we are emperor.

[*Giving a sign to Harlequin, who runs out, he turns to Altoum*]

O Sire—elect!
Before the ominous gong sounds in mine ears
That ushers me unto oblivious rags
To stroll the world again, let me rejoice
That you have turned your wrath from this brave youth
Upon *my* humble head.—Congratulations!
And with exchange of courtesies, I pray you
Felicitate me and these fellow-players
On the happy curtain of our comedy.

[*At his gesture, Punchinello and Pantaloon run to the curtain at back*]

ALTOUM

Say rather—tragedy.

CAPO.

We stand corrected:

Or say—romance, where true love laughs through tears:

Name it Romance, and grant us your applause.

[*Punchinello and Pantaloon draw the curtain, revealing an oriental altar, with idol, beside which stand two priests*]

ALTOUM

What's there?

CAPO.

The altar for our ceremony:

The Wedding of the Princess and the Beggar.

[*Reënter Harlequin, bringing in Barak, who rushes to Calaf and embraces him*]

BARAK

My prince!

CALAF

[*Overwhelmed*]

Barak—old friend!

TURANDOT

[*To Zelima*]

Look, look, 'tis he!

My beggar's gaffer.

ALTOUM

[*Before whom Harlequin presents three tokens*]

What are these?

CAPO.

Our trophies:

The secret of your daughter's malady—

[*Leading Calaf bewildered before Turandot*]

Lady, receive them with your heart's desire:

A ring, a rose, a beggar's wallet.

TURANDOT

You—

Are *you* my beggar?

CALAF

[*Taking from Barak his old cloak*]

I am he who won

In Astrakhan—this rose, at Pekin gate—

This ring, and in this ragged beggar's cloak

You once did smile upon, I now depart.

TURANDOT

Stay, love—*You* are my noblest in the world!

[*Calaf turns in wonder and kneels to her. She bends and embraces him. A great gong resounds*]

CAPO.

[*Presenting his crown to Altoum*]

My liege, I abdicate. And you applaud?

ALTOUM

Yea, marvel, Capo. Kingdoms will I give
To these your fellows.

THE MASKERS

[*Bowing Venetian*]

Hail!

ALTOUM

And to yourself yourself—
Whate'er you ask for.

CAPO.

Then, my liege and lady,
I beg—this withered rose.

CALAF

[*Giving it to him*]

Only a flower?

CAPO.

Lovers, that lives beyond its little hour
In memory.—Adieu!—My players, rule
Your kingdoms still in masks.—Now for the world!

[*Tossing his gorgeous emperor's cloak to Harlequin, he springs away in his tattered motley*]

TURANDOT

[*Calls after him*]

What seek you there?

CAPO.

[*Kissing to her and Calaf the withered rose*]

More roses and romance!

Curtain

END OF PLAY

APPENDIX

TURANDOT'S DREAM

In the acted performance of this play, the third act commences with a scene which sets forth, wholly in pantomime, a dream of Turandot, representing—by suggestions of mystic light and sound—the state of her distracted mind, trying to solve the riddle of Keedur Khan.

The pantomime takes place in two imaginative settings—a mountain top and an oriental street—blending the one into the other.

Out of darkness first appears the outline of the dark summit, against a blue-gray radiance of sky. Etched upon this Zelima enters, like a shadow-phantom, beckoning. Following her to strange music Turandot appears, unsubstantial as shadow, painted opaque on the glowing background, like some silhouetted, featureless figure on an ancient vase, imbued as by magic with motion and antique gesture.

Bowing in awe above the brink of darkness, the figure of Turandot is led downward (and forward) into obscuring mists, tinged with green lights and gules. Out of the mist, voices—shrill, bizarre, bell-toned, menacing, mysterious—echo the words: "Khan, Keedur Khan, Khan, Khan!"

While the female forms grope below, the figure of Capocomico now appears on the summit, beckoning to his four maskers, whose shadow-forms gesticulate weirdly toward Turandot.

"Reveal, O Lady: What is he—

His true-born name,

His father's fame—?"

Through the interpretive music, the teasing words of the riddle are chanted by the varied voices, amid strange hiatuses filled with mocking laughter.

Lastly, alone, appears the shadow form of Calaf, who follows the Maskers downward into the mist, searching with arms outgroped toward Turandot.

There, as the unreal forms pass and disappear, the silhouette of Capocomico stands fluting on the mountain top, while below echoes the basso and falsetto laughter of the Maskers, and the low taunting cry: "Keedur Khan!"

As this tableau shuts in darkness, there comes vaguely to light in the foreground a street scene. Here, at a gateway, beggars with yokes are huddled; before the gate, a moving frieze of dream figures, noiseless, pass fantastically:

Chinese soldiers, high stepping; Turandot again, downcast, gliding like a captive with Zelima; Calaf, swift searching in pursuit; the Maskers, lithe, grotesque, pointing after him; rearguarded by Capocomico—blithely dominant in gesture, triumphant with fantasy.

Last of the dream images he also fades in darkness, out of which rise the merry strains of a chorus:

"O Lady, Lady, let fall your tears

No more, no more for foolish fears,

But let in your blithe playfellow——"

and Turandot, sobbing beside Zelima on her bench in the harem, awakes from her haunting dream of Keedur Khan.

Zelima bends over her.

"Alas, my lady, what ails you? You cried in your swoon!"

The merry voices of the Maskers outside sing louder.

"Oh, I have dreamed, Zelima! Drive them away!"

Thus follows the first spoken scene of Act Third, as here printed.

As acted, the stage management and lighting of this pantomime have been movingly devised by Mr. J. C. Huffman.

Here in description its visionary quality can only be suggested.

---

1. Since the date of the commission for my play, the translation of "Turandot" by Jethro Bithell has been published in America by Duffield & Company, New York, so that the Gossi-Schiller-Voellmueller dramatic version of the folk-tale is thus made available for English readers.

2. See Appendix.

Milton Keynes UK
Ingram Content Group UK Ltd.
UKHW042300170324
439575UK00004B/379